For Jackson

Best Wishes
B
RAAAAAAAAR!!

CANADIAN MONSTER CLUB

THE SUMMER PICNIC

BY TROY TOWNSIN
ILLUSTRATED BY TRISH GLAB

FOR EMILIA, FELIX, LUCAS AND ALEXANDRA –
OUR VERY OWN AND MUCH LOVED AMAZING CANADIAN MONSTERS.

Printed in Canada by Friesens
Library and Archives Canada Cataloguing in Publication

Townsin, Troy, 1975-, author, illustrator
       Canadian monster club : the summer picnic / by Troy Townsin;
illustrated by Patricia Glab.

ISBN 978-0-9868892-8-8 (bound)

       1. Monsters--Canada--Juvenile fiction. I. Glab, Patricia, 1976-,
illustrator II. Title.

PS8639.O998C366 2015   jC813'.6   C2014-905580-3

Check out more great Canadian titles at www.amooseinamapletree.com

Being a monster can be a very lonely and very boring job.

So every year on the 1st of July
(while the humans are busy with Canada Day parties and parades),
monsters from all over Canada are excited to get together in a

TOP SECRET

meeting place
for the
Canadian Monster Club
summer picnic.

They come by air -
beating their powerful wings,

swirling and twirling,
through fluffy white clouds.

They come by water –

up winding rivers and
babbling streams
or surfing in on
mighty ocean waves.

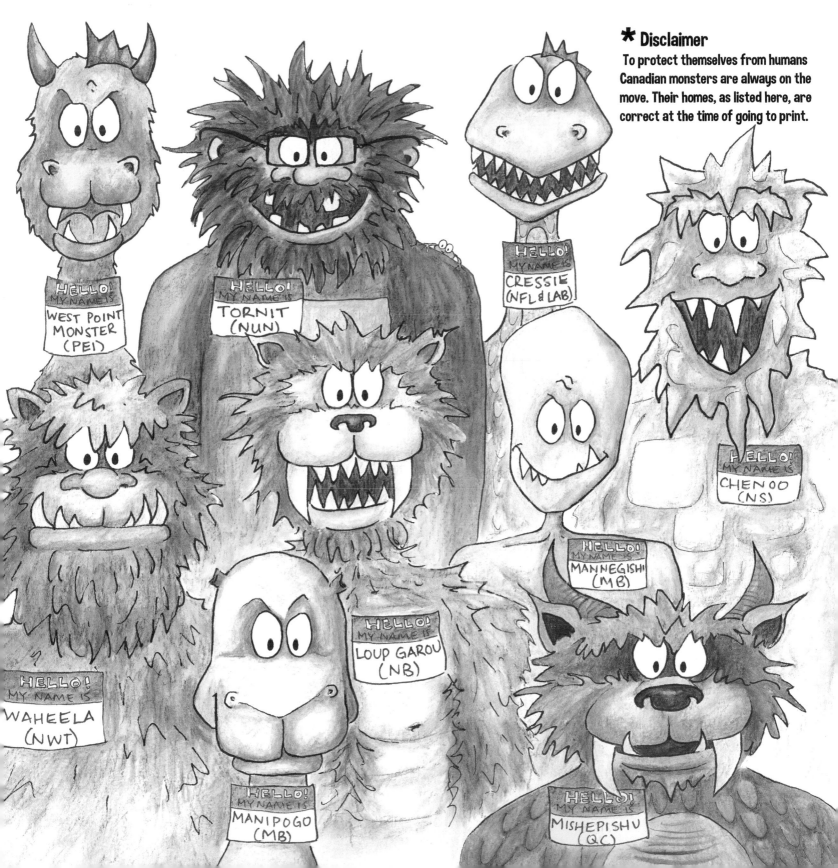

HELLO! MY NAME IS WEST POINT MONSTER (PEI)

HELLO! MY NAME IS TORNIT (NUN)

HELLO! MY NAME IS CRESSIE (NFL & LAB)

HELLO! MY NAME IS CHENOO (NS)

HELLO! MY NAME IS WAHEELA (NWT)

HELLO! MY NAME IS MANNEGISHI (MB)

HELLO! MY NAME IS LOUP GAROU (NB)

HELLO! MY NAME IS MANIPOGO (MB)

HELLO! MY NAME IS MISHEPISHU (QC)

When everyone has arrived, Sasquatch roars

"LET THE GAMES BEGIN!"

and they all sing the

HORRIBLE

monster anthem,
frightening off the animals
for kilometres around.

Monster games played at the picnic are: Hide and Go Seek,
(because monsters are experts at hiding)

CAN YOU FIND
17 MONSTERS?

9 McINTOSH APPLES

1 HOCKEY STICK

7 SASQUATCH FOOTPRINTS

4 THUNDERBIRD EGGS

3 BUCKETS MAPLE SYRUP

5 LOGS

4 FROGS

2 CAMERAS

1 CANOE

2 CANADA GEESE

egg and spoon races,
(using Thunderbird eggs)

and best of all -
SWAMP HOCKEY!

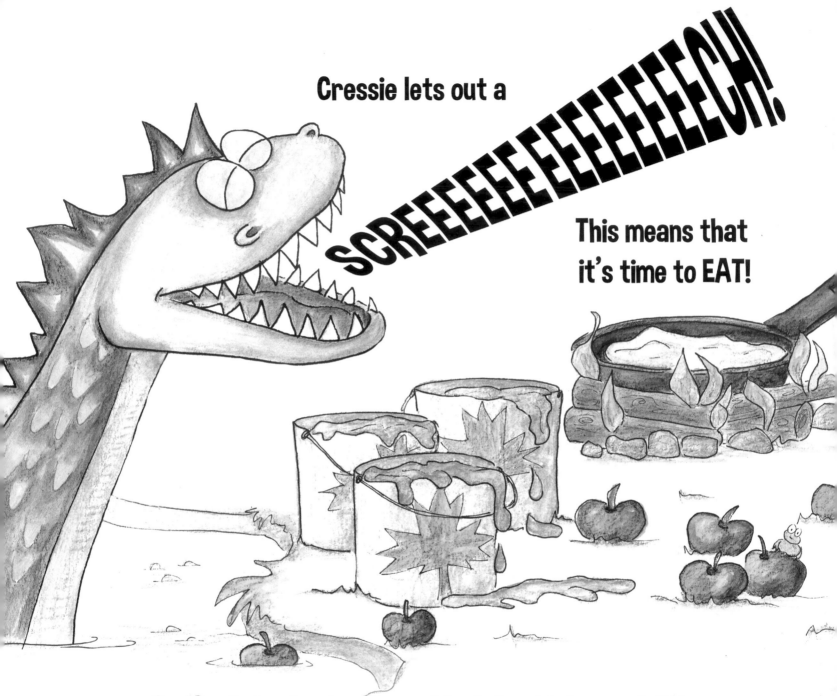

Cressie lets out a SCREEEEEEEEEEEEEECH!

This means that it's time to EAT!

Some of the foods you and I might think are delicious -
buckets of gooey maple syrup, crunchy McIntosh apples,
and fire-baked bannock with wild honey.

But other foods would make your stomach turn -
blackfly pie, moose poo-tine,
and banana slug sundaes.

BURRRP!

MUNCHCRUNCHMUNCH

Monsters have no table manners
and before long,
the air is filled with
the disgusting sounds of
slurping
and
burping,
munching
and
crunching,
laughing
and
barfing.

"FOOD FIGHT!" yells Loup-Garou,
as she throws a plate of salmon heads at Manipogo,
who has her nose stuck in a jar of blackberry jam.

Everyone joins the wild ruckus.
Chenoo spurts a mouthful of spoiled beaver milk
into Mannegishi's face
as the monsters sing the food fight song.

The last and most important event of the day is
THE FRIGHTENING.
This year it is Mishepishu's turn to scare a human.

Together the monsters choose a human to scare.
They make sure that there are no cameras or phones nearby
so that no pictures can be taken.
Very, very quietly, the monsters sing their song.

Eh! Eh! Eh! Ooh La La!
Monster Club of CA - NA - DA
Humans, bears and even moose
run from monsters on the loose!
RAAAAAR!

"AAAAAAARRRRRRRGGGGGGHHHHHHH!"

screams the extremely frightened human,
running away as fast as his little legs will carry him.

"AU REVOIR!"

waves Mishepishu.

The monsters roll around on the ground laughing.
What a **PERFECT DAY** they have had.

When he gets home, the poor human tells everyone what he has seen -

his mom, the newspapers, the TV news, and even the Prime Minister of Canada!

But, of course, nobody believes him because he could not get a picture.

As the sun sets, the monsters say their monster good-byes
and give their monster hugs.

Getting ready to head home across Canada to their
monster caves,

holes,

craters,

and lakes,

they sing one last
monster song.

About the Author

Troy Townsin is a proud new Canadian!

Born in Melbourne, Australia, he worked as an actor and playwright before embarking on a round-the-world backpacking extravaganza taking him to six continents. Troy is a man of many talents and has had a wide variety of jobs. He has been a Stage Manager in Australia, a Teacher-Trainer in Thailand, a Beverage Manager in the UK, an Information Officer for the United Nations and is currently a Columnist for CBC Radio in Canada. Troy has won several awards for his writing including a prestigious 'Travel Writer of the Year' award from TNT Magazine UK and four Gourmand World Cookbook Awards.

Troy fell in love with a Canadian girl, married her and then fell in love with Canada, his new home. Other illustrated titles that have been authored by Troy include the best-selling Moose in a Maple Tree collection.

About the Illustrator

Born in St. Catharines, Ontario, Trish has also lived in Montreal and Toronto where she attended university for Music and Environmental Studies. She loves discovering the culture of Canada's largest cities and has a deep appreciation for the remote natural areas of this country. In addition to her job in International Education, Trish is a much sought after Wedding and Portrait Photographer. She is a creative genius and her talent shines through across a diverse array of media. Some of her amazing creations include colourful canvases, spectacular cakes, extraordinary tuques and knitted animals and outrageous furniture designs and décor. Canadian Monster Club is her first book of illustrations.

Trish Glab lives in Victoria, BC with her two children, her husband, a dog and a cat.

www.amooseinamapletree.com